700024175637

D0310175

for Rosie

and Leo

WORCESTERSHIRE COUNTY
COUNCIL

563

BfS	12 May 2003
	£ 10.99

First published 2003 by Walker Books Ltd
87 Vauxhall Walk, London SE11 5HJ

2 4 6 8 10 9 7 5 3 1

© 2003 Jessica Spanyol

The right of Jessica Spanyol to be identified as author/illustrator of this work
has been asserted by her in accordance with the Copyright, Designs and Patents Act 1988

This book has been typeset in Garamond Book Educational and Spanyol Bold

Printed in Italy

All rights reserved. No part of this book may be reproduced, transmitted
or stored in an information retrieval system in any form or by any means, graphic,
electronic or mechanical, including photocopying, taping and recording,
without prior written permission from the publisher.

British Library Cataloguing in Publication Data:
a catalogue record for this book is available
from the British Library

ISBN 0-7445-9607-6

Carlo Likes Colours

Jessica Spanyol

WALKER BOOKS
AND SUBSIDIARIES
LONDON · BOSTON · SYDNEY

Carlo sees yellow in the field.

haystack

sunflower

beak

wheat

chick

chick

Carlo sees red
in the street.

fire extinguisher

off   on

fire engine

strawberry

rose

Carlo and Crackers see black at the bandstand.

blackbird

Crackers

hole

crow

acorn

owl

Carlo and Nevil see brown in the woods.

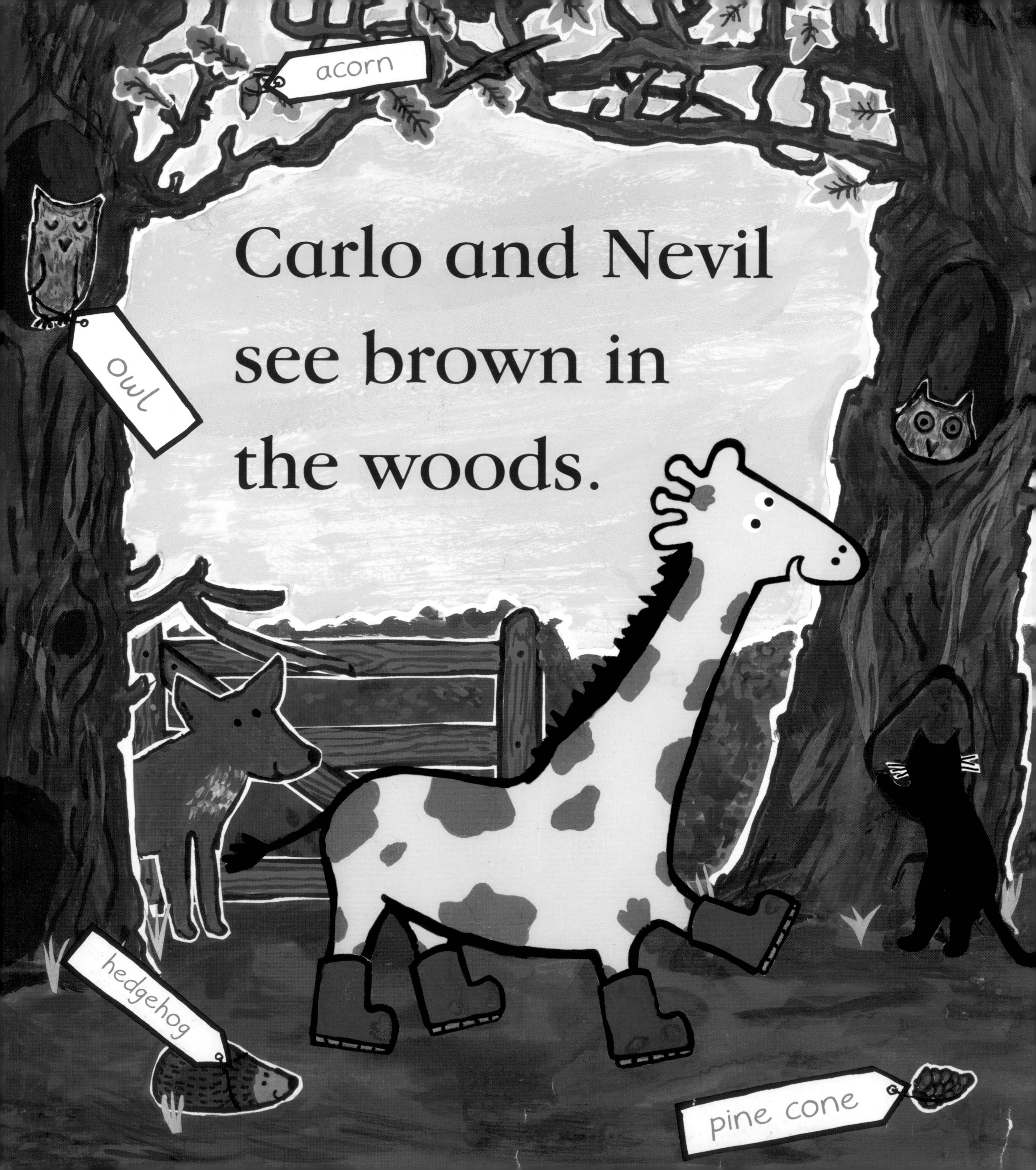

hedgehog

pine cone

Carlo and Sandra see green by the stream.

grass

lizard

grass snake

grasshopper

caterpillar

Carlo sees white at the wedding.

dove

jasmine

confetti

plum

Carlo sees purple in the vegetable garden.

cabbages

Carlo sees orange at the café.

marigolds

ginger cat

orange juice

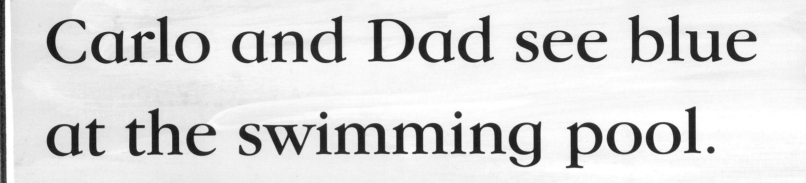

Carlo and Dad see blue
at the swimming pool.

sky

splash

splash

pool

ROSIE'S

milkshake

Bab's Baby Boutique

Carlo and Mum see pink at the shops.

candyfloss

carnation

worm

ice cream

tutu

ballet shoe

pig

cheek

flamingo

Carlo likes colours very much.

And he loves
beeping!